PUFFIN BOOK

JOSEPH'S BEAR

Some day, Joseph dreamed, he was going to catch himself a rabbit, a squirrel, a fox, or even a deer, for a pet. He would love any of those creatures, and it would make up for the way the other children laughed at his dreamy ways, and his lack of success at school.

Then one day the unbelievable happened – a little man arrived at their settlement with a big shambling brown dancing bear, and he *gave* the bear to Joseph!

Joseph had his pet now, and a better one than even he could have dreamed of, but little shivers crept all over him as he thought what his parents would say when he brought home such an enormous and hungry animal. The bear was just what he wanted, but it was more than doubtful whether he would be allowed to keep it . . .

Evelyn Davies had several short stories published in children's comics during the 1950s. She has a son and a daughter, and has been for some time the licensee of an Inn in Hampshire.

EVELYN DAVIES

JOSEPH'S BEAR

Illustrated by Jane Paton

PUFFIN BOOKS

in association with
Hamish Hamilton Children's Books

Puffin Books, Penguin Books Ltd, Harmondsworth, Middlesex, England
Viking Penguin Inc., 40 West 23rd Street, New York, New York 10010, U.S.A.
Penguin Books Australia Ltd, Ringwood, Victoria, Australia
Penguin Books Canada Limited, 2801 John Street, Markham, Ontario, Canada L3R 1B4
Penguin Books (N.Z.) Ltd, 182–190 Wairau Road, Auckland 10, New Zealand

—

First published by Hamish Hamilton Children's Books 1975
Published in Puffin Books 1977
Reprinted 1981, 1986

—

—

Printed and bound in Great Britain by
Cox & Wyman Ltd, Reading
Set in Monotype Plantin

For Toby

Contents

Chapter One

In the School House

SOMETHING was tickling Joseph's ear. He was watching a spider crawling over the school house ceiling. He could see the sky through the chinks in the wooden slats. If he screwed up his eyes it looked as though the ceiling was streaked with paint – bright, summer-sky, blue paint.

He could smell the good out-door smells that came in through those chinks. He could smell meadow grass and waving corn and freshly-turned earth. If he breathed in real hard he could smell wood smoke mixed with the faint, delicate smell of wild rice. It was the time of the rice harvest and in the marshy lakes in the dip of the valley Indians were gathering the tall, bending rice and parching it over slow

9

fires in readiness for the coming winter.

Oh, how he wished he was down there in the valley instead of in the hot school house. Why, he could even taste the sweet, smoky flavour of that wild rice, feel the hard grains between his teeth just as he had on that first September day when they had come to settle here.

He had only been four years old then and it was six years ago but he remembered it as if it was yesterday. There had just been him and Mother and Father and Grandmother and Grandfather, little Jessie, his baby sister, hadn't been born yet, and it seemed they were the only people in all the world under that big, wide, blue sky. He had been a little afraid.

Then the Indians had come. He hadn't seen them coming. Suddenly they were there. They had put a leather pouch filled with the long, dark brown grains of rice by the fire without saying a word and disappeared as silently as they had come. It was their way of offering friendship Father said. Grandmother had said, 'That settles it. Here we stay.' And here they were, a tiny settlement of just three families,

for the next year Uncle Isaac and Aunt Lyddie and Cousin Ham and Cousin Shad and Cousin Hannah had travelled west in their covered wagon to join them. Little Jessie was two years old now.

The spider had stopped to eat a fly, now it was continuing its slow, upside down journey. Joseph eyed it scornfully. How stupid that spider was, crawling over the school house ceiling instead of outside under that bright, summer-blue sky. It was just over Cousin Ham's head. Cousin Ham didn't see it, his head was bent over his school book. Cousin Ham sat in front of Joseph.

Now the spider was just over Cousin Shad's head. Cousin Shad didn't see it, his head was bent over his school book. Cousin Shad sat in front of Cousin Ham.

Now the spider was just over Cousin Hannah's head. Cousin Hannah didn't see it, her head was bent over her school book. Cousin Hannah sat in front of Cousin Shad at the top of the class – in the seat by the window.

If she looked up, if she looked out of that

window Cousin Hannah could see the smoke from the Indian fires. She could see the meadows and cornfields, the hills and rivers and forests, the bright, summer-blue sky. But she didn't look up.

How stupid Cousin Hannah was looking at her school book instead of out of the window. Joseph glanced scornfully at her bent head. Oh, but how he envied her. How he wished one day he would be chosen to sit in the seat by the window, but, of course, he never would. He would never be clever enough to earn a place at the top of the class.

One whole, long year Cousin Ham had sat there. Another year Cousin Shad sat there, and now Cousin Hannah was sitting there, but always Joseph sat behind them all.

He sighed, and now it wasn't a spidery feeling on his ear. It was a smooth, soft feeling. Smooth as a rabbit's paw, soft as a squirrel's tail. There were rabbits and squirrels in the forests, and shy foxes and deer and furry opossums hanging upside down by their tails. There were silent owls looking for all the world

13

like a part of the tree they were sitting on, and lizards and shrews and hurrying, scurrying beetles, their shards shining like silver as they moved through a shaft of sunlight. He had seen them. But most likely Cousin Ham and Cousin Shad and Cousin Hannah didn't even know they were there.

One day he was going to catch himself a rabbit or a squirrel or a fox, a deer even, for a pet. Joseph smiled thinking about it. How he would love any one of those creatures. A deer to follow him wherever he went, a fox to play with, a rabbit to fondle, a squirrel to sit on his shoulder. Why, he could feel that squirrel on his shoulder now, feel its soft, bushy tail curled around his ear, smoothing his cheek, and Joseph bent his head, loving that gentle squirrel. He lifted his hand with an imaginary tit-bit. Something hard rapped his knuckles. Something prodded his neck. His head jerked forward. He gave a little squeal. Now he knew what had been tickling his ear. Not a spider. Not a squirrel's tail – Uncle Isaac's cane! Uncle Isaac was the schoolmaster. His long

cane had a hard knob on one end and a squirrel's tail on the other and if the children weren't paying attention to their lessons, if they were dreaming over their books, Uncle Isaac prodded them sharply with the hard knob and tickled them awake with the squirrel's tail.

Now everyone knew Joseph had been dreaming again. They turned around and giggled. All except Cousin Hannah. Cousin Hannah was looking out of the window! She was standing up and staring. Staring and staring out of the window.

She said in a scared, squeaky little voice they could hardly hear. 'There's a bear outside.'

Chapter Two

The Dancing Bear

COUSIN HANNAH was right. There was a bear outside – a big brown bear, lumbering straight towards the school house.

Everyone crowded to the window, bobbing up and down to see over each other's heads. They were so busy looking at the big brown bear they didn't notice a little man in fringed buckskins and a coon-skin hat until he was standing right beside that bear, shouting and waving, shaking his fist in the bear's face. Then they held their breath. They almost stopped breathing they were so afraid what that big bear would do to the little man.

And what did she do? She sat down! She sat on her haunches and scratched the back of her head with one of her big furry paws.

It was so quiet in the school house they could clearly hear the scraping sound of the bear's long claws scratching her hard old head.

Now the little man in the coon-skin hat stopped shouting. He stopped shaking his fists. He pulled a yellow handkerchief from around his neck and wiped his face. He sat on the ground beside the bear. He tipped his coon-skin hat over his eyes and scratched the back of his head. Everyone laughed. They laughed very hard, they were so relieved the bear wasn't fierce.

Now lessons were forgotten. Everyone rushed out of the school house and stood in a ring looking at that big bear and the little man sitting scratching the back of their heads.

And now here came Father looking very worried and very concerned at having a bear loose in the settlement.

And Grandfather came, and Grandmother, and Aunt Lyddie, and Mother with little Jessie who was too small for school clinging to her skirt and dancing up and down very curious and very excited to see that big bear.

They all came. Everyone left what they had been doing and came running to see the bear. Now they stopped. They stood and stared very surprised to see her and the little man in the fringed buckskins and coon-skin hat, sitting there calmly scratching the back of their heads.

How surprised that little man was suddenly to see all those people around him. He quickly jumped to his feet. He pulled a reed pipe from one of his big patch pockets and played a tune on it. At once the bear rose up on her hind

legs. Everyone gasped and hastily took a step back. Oh, how tall she was now. But not fierce. Oh, no not at all fierce. Clumsily she swayed to the ragged tune, awkwardly she swung first one leg then the other, slowly she raised her front paws above her head, unsteadily she turned around and around and around on her big flat feet – she was dancing!

Everyone stared – a bear dancing! Who ever heard of such a thing! They couldn't believe their eyes. Then they smiled. Little Jessie chuckled and jumped up and down harder than ever. Faster went the tune, faster and louder. Faster danced the bear, faster and faster. Everyone laughed, they laughed and clapped. What fun it was to see that big bear dance.

Joseph tilted back on his heels. He tipped his head right back to look up at her. Surely there never was a bear so big. Surely she was bigger than any bear in the forest, but thinner, her ribs could be easily seen; and her coat was not thick and shining like the wild bears' coats. It was dull and matted, pieces of briars and dead twigs were tangled in it. They looked as if they had been tangled there a very long time.

Joseph was filled with pity for that clumsily dancing bear. And then suddenly he was filled with anger, too. Round the bear's neck was a wide, sore mark where a too tight collar had rubbed her skin raw. There were other marks like bands of red ribbon round each of her hind legs from hobbles that had eaten into the flesh.

Joseph clenched his fists. His face burned, he shivered, he went hot and cold he was that angry. He wanted to shout at the little man in the coon-skin hat to stop playing on his reed pipe, but he couldn't make a sound. He wanted to rush up and grab that big bear and run and run with her to the forest where she belonged, but he couldn't move. He bit his lip. How every one would laugh. Why, he wouldn't get two steps before he was brought back.

He closed his eyes so that he couldn't see the clumsy, dancing bear, couldn't see the raw marks, the tangled briars.

He heard Father say to the little man, 'You and the bear can spend the night in the barn. There is plenty of clean straw, you'll be warm and comfortable and after a good night's sleep you will be fit to travel on in the morning.'

Now the music stopped. Joseph felt himself jostled as everyone moved back, then carried forward as laughing and chattering they followed the bear and the little man to the big barn.

The little man pulled off his boots and stretched out on a pile of straw, grinning his delight. The bear scrabbled in the straw, sniffing and snuffling at it, throwing it up in the air like a playful puppy, her heavy chain clanking on the barn floor.

Joseph's eyes narrowed. Suddenly he smiled. You almost would have thought he was happy to see that big bear chained up in the barn beside the little man.

Chapter Three

Joseph's Plan

OH, no, Joseph wasn't happy. He wasn't at all happy that the big bear was chained up in the barn. But he was happy with his thoughts, with the wonderful plan that had suddenly come into his head. When it was dark, when everyone was in bed and asleep, he decided, he would take that bear to the forest and leave her there to live with the wild bears.

How impatient he was. How long it took for the sun to go down. And when at last it did slide behind the hills there was the big round moon to take its place and it was as light as day again; and tired as they were after a hard day's work no one was in a hurry to go to bed.

Lying fully clothed on his mattress of corn husks it seemed to Joseph the voices would never stop. What could they find to talk about so long into the night? The voices, the smell of his freshly stuffed mattress made him sleepy. His head nodded, his eyes closed, he almost fell asleep. He sat up with a jerk. It was quiet!

Joseph forced himself to wait. He counted slowly on his fingers. He counted up to one hundred. He had never done that before, not right up to one hundred. He jumped out of bed.

A shaft of moonlight as he opened the barn door showed him the bear asleep in a corner, her chain tied firmly to an upright pole. The little man snored softly in another corner. Stealthily Joseph unwound the chain and gave it a little tug. The bear grunted but at once rose clumsily to her feet and obediently followed him to the door, shaking the straw from her back. The little man slept on.

Joseph smiled; he had been afraid she might not want to come with him, might not want to leave her master. He gave her a crust of bread he had saved from supper and she ambled after him, happily snuffling in his pockets for more.

It would have been easier and quicker to

walk straight across the meadows but in the moonlight they would too easily have been seen should anyone happen to glance out of a window. It took twice as long going around the edge, keeping to the shadows of the bluffs, and the bear was in no hurry. It had been warm and stuffy in the barn, now she was enjoying the cool night breezes, turning her head from side to side, drawing in great breaths of air or snatching at berries on the low bushes. Sometimes stopping altogether just to sit down and scratch.

Joseph was impatient. Over the ridge in the centre of the forest bright, fast-flowing rivers fell out of the mountains, surging and foaming over the boulders, the spray rising like a thin curtain laced with misty rainbows. Here the great salmon that had so bravely fought their way up to their spawning beds in the spring would now be making their way back to their breeding grounds, and the wild bears, fat, lazy and overfed, would carelessly flip them from the water with their paws and eat them more from habit than hunger. This was where

Joseph had planned to take the little man's bear, but it was a long way and she would not be hurried. She rooted among the fallen leaves for acorns and little three-cornered beech nuts, sometimes pushing her long snout into hollow trees and bringing it out dripping with sweet wild honey; and no amount of coaxing or tugging would persuade her to move on until she was ready.

Joseph glanced at a streak of light low in the eastern sky. Soon day would break. An owl hooted softly and settled down to sleep the day away. Now the birds were stirring, calling softly, fluttering and preening high in the branches, gradually raising their voices, flying lower, singing louder, singing, singing until all the forest was awake. The streak in the eastern sky had brightened.

Joseph was desperate. He let the bear's long chain slip from his fingers, she wandered ahead. He would never get her to the mountain falls now. It was too late. He stamped his foot with anger and disappointment, uncertain and undecided. If only she had hurried – just a little.

If she hadn't been so greedy—! He tugged the chain fiercely and she winced away from him, surprised at the unexpected harsh treatment. Now he was ashamed. Suddenly he had an idea. He didn't have time to take the bear to the falls but she could take herself. Instinct would lead her to the wild bears and if he ran all the way back he would be in bed again before he was missed. He slipped the collar from her neck and feeling she was free she ambled off, pushing her way through a tangle of undergrowth. Joseph watched her for a minute but she didn't turn back. He gathered up the chain and ran.

By the time he reached the barn he was so out of breath he had to lean against the wall and get his breath back before he could go in. The little man was still snoring. Carefully Joseph fastened the bear's collar to look as if she had slipped her head through it and escaped, then he dropped the chain in the straw and tiptoed out of the barn.

In a few minutes he was in bed. The next thing he knew Mother was calling him to get up.

Chapter Four

That Stupid Bear

AT first he thought he had been dreaming. He was muddled with sleep. He hadn't really taken the bear to the forest. Joseph rubbed his eyes. Perhaps there hadn't been a bear at all, or a little man in a coon-skin hat. Bears didn't dance on the end of chains. Yes, he had been dreaming.

He heard Cousin Ham and Cousin Shad calling as they ran past his window. 'Joseph, Joseph, come and see the bear.' And Cousin Hannah's little worried voice, 'Wait for me. Wait. Wait.'

He jumped out of bed. He was fully dressed. He hadn't been dreaming! He smiled. How surprised they would be when they found the bear had gone.

He took his time pretending to be dressing. He walked slowly to the barn, pleased with himself, and edged his way through the group gathered around the barn door. He looked at the little man's surprised, puzzled face. He looked at all the surprised, puzzled faces around him. He looked at – his eyes popped, his mouth dropped open. He looked at – that big brown bear sitting in the middle of the barn! He HAD been dreaming. He hadn't taken the bear to the forest.

He caught sight of the chain lying in the straw just as he had left it, the collar fastened to look as if the bear had slipped her head through it and wandered away. Now he was confused. He didn't know what was real and what was a dream any more.

The little man picked up the collar and chain, 'Must have slipped her collar somehow,' he said. 'Though I don't know how she managed to open the door. I'm sure I fastened it securely.' He shook his head, pondering. 'Ah, well, perhaps I didn't. I was very tired last night. Slept like a log. Anyway she didn't go far and when I woke up this morning there she was sitting outside waiting for me to open the door and let her back in.'

Joseph stared. She had come back. That stupid bear had come back! He couldn't believe it. He had taken her to the forest. He had given her her freedom, but she had come back. By now she could have been far away, deep in the forest, growing fat on berries and nuts and fish from the mountain rivers, romping and playing with the wild bears. Soon the sore places on her neck and legs would be healing, her coat growing thick and long.

Joseph turned away. He couldn't bear to look at her. Anger and disappointment overwhelmed him.

Uncle Isaac was ringing the school bell. Blindly Joseph pushed his way out of the barn. He ran all the way to the school house. He was the first one there. Well, let that bear be hobbled and chained, he thought fiercely, let her dance on the end of a chain for the rest of her life. As if he cared.

Chapter Five

A Bear for a Pet

JOSEPH tried not to think of the bear. He tried very hard. He didn't so much as glance towards the school house window in case he should catch a glimpse of her going past. He kept his head bent over his school book.

He had said he didn't care but, of course, he did. He hurt inside when he thought of the sore places on that bear's neck.

By the time school was out the bear and the little man had gone on their way. Joseph climbed to the rim of the bluff that over-shadowed the settlement and looked all about him. He looked for the bear and the little man.

The rim was so high, you could see so far and so much it was like sitting on top of the world. Far below, the swallows flew in graceful circles, their chestnut bibs catching the sun as they dived and swooped and turned, and dived again.

A hawk dropped silently from an empty sky on some unsuspecting prey. Its outstretched wings almost brushed Joseph's face. He listened for its triumphant cry, but no sound came. Maybe this time the hawk had missed. Maybe. Just this once!

By now the bear and the little man were far away – on the next farm or settlement perhaps. The little man piping his thin tuneless notes, the bear dancing for her supper. She was stupid, but she couldn't help it. She had been brought up in captivity, never known freedom, never roamed wild and free.

Joseph moved back from the edge of the bluff and looked down into a deep gulch. He rubbed his eyes. He didn't believe what he saw down there. He saw the bear, and the little man in the coon-skin hat, and the little man was digging! Down there in that barren, creek-seamed gulch the little man was digging. Frantically striking the hard rock surface. The ring of his spade echoed in the still air.

Joseph stared. What was he doing? Nothing grew up here. No one came here to dig. Now he was shovelling the dry loose earth into a big wire sieve and swirling it round and round as though he was winnowing grain – separating the husks from the grain. The little man was mad for sure.

Now Joseph was filled with curiosity. He scrambled clumsily down into the gulch. The little man looked up and rested on his shovel waiting for him. He didn't really look mad, just hot from hard work.

'Looking for gold, son,' he said, seeing the question in Joseph's eyes. 'I'm on my way to Bright Water Valley, they tell me there's a fortune to be dug out of the rocks there. I thought maybe there might well be gold in these hills, too. You ever heard tell of it?'

Joseph shook his head, he wasn't really listening to the little man, he was looking at the bear. Her ribs showed like iron bars round her thin body.

'No one ever dug for gold up here, have they?' The little man bent and examined the rough wall of the gulch.

'Reckon they haven't,' he said, answering his own question, 'leastways if they have they didn't find it or there'd be more than you few folks living down there. Reckon I'm just wasting my time.' He tipped up the sieve scattering earth over the dry creek bed. The bear snuffled it hopefully for food.

'She's hungry,' Joseph said.

'Reckon she is, she takes a lot of feeding, there's little enough for me let alone the bear.' The little man snapped his knife shut. 'Guess

we'd better get going.' He stuffed the sieve in an old bulging sack, threw it over his shoulder with the shovel and bent to pick up the bear's chain. The shovel clattered to the ground. It fell on the bear's foot. The bear jumped sideways, she bumped against the little man. The little man yelled. He dropped the sack, the sieve fell out, a black kettle fell out, a tin mug fell out, a loaf of stale bread rolled in the dust. The little man grabbed for it, the bear grabbed for it, both at the same time. The bear reached it first. She stuffed it in her mouth. She swallowed it in one gulp.

The little man exploded. He turned first red then white then purple with rage. He yelled and shouted at that bear. He almost burst with anger.

'That stupid bear,' he screamed. 'How I got mixed up with such a stupid bear I'll never know.'

'She's hungry,' Joseph said again.

'Hungry!' snorted the little man. 'She'll be a lot hungrier. Here she's just eaten all the food we had and goodness knows how long it'll be before we get any more. Darn me if she isn't the stupidest bear.'

'She can't help being hungry,' Joseph said.

The little man looked sideways at Joseph. His eyes narrowed with hidden thoughts. He thought about them a long time. He said at last, 'Say, how'd you like to have her? – for a pet? She's a real nice bear, really. Can't help being hungry, can she?' He wheedled. 'Needs a settled home she does. All this roaming about's no good for a bear.'

'Have her? For my very own?' Joseph couldn't take it in. Why, in all his wildest dreams he had never thought of having a bear for a pet. He smoothed her great shaggy head. He couldn't take his eyes off her. He stroked her poor thin body. 'I'll take care of her,' he whispered. 'I'll be good to her, I promise.' He turned around but already the little man was disappearing around the end of the gulch.

Half-way down the bluff Joseph remembered Mother and Father. He stood still and little shivers crept all over him as he thought what

they would say when he brought home a bear
for a pet.

Mother said nothing. She just stood and
stared.

Father said nothing. For a minute he didn't
quite take in what Joseph was saying. He was
talking so fast, telling everything at once,
jumbling the words, mixing them together. He
wasn't telling it very well, he was so worried
what Mother and Father would say. He knew
what they would say.

Father said, 'A bear! Of course you can't
have a bear for a pet. Really Joseph, as if we
haven't enough mouths to feed already. Just
you turn right around this minute and take her
back to that little man. This very minute. D'ye
hear me?'

Oh yes, Joseph heard all right and he bit his
lip. He wanted so badly to beg and plead to be
allowed to keep that bear, but he didn't dare
when Father spoke in that voice. He turned
right around but before he had taken one step
he heard Mother say, 'It's nearly dusk, Joseph
will never catch the little man now, not before

44

nightfall, he would just get lost in the hills. The little man is sure to rest up for the night and if Joseph sets off good and early he will find him before he goes on his way in the morning.'

'Very well,' Father said. This was good sense. 'In the morning then. FIRST thing in the morning.'

Chapter Six

Grandmother's Red Skirt

NOW this was the day Mother and Grandmother and Aunt Lyddie did their washing. As soon as it was light they each took a big iron pot and a round wooden tub filled with clothes down to the river.

Here they soon had three fires burning. They built the fires in a ring of stones, filled the iron pots with water and hung them on tripods to heat over the flames.

They liked washdays. They chattered and gossiped and planned and arranged things while they scrubbed and rub-a-dubbed in the warm soapy water, laughing and giggling when the soap bubbles floated up and burst on the tips of their noses.

Joseph saw them as he crossed the river by

the big boulders that made stepping stones through the fast flowing water. He was up early, too. He was taking the bear back to the little man. He hadn't slept for thinking about it. He had cried in the dark.

He glanced wistfully to where Mother and Grandmother and Aunt Lyddie were doing their washing. Mother had saved him from taking the bear back last night. Now if she were to talk to Father. If Mother were to ask him – but she was lost in a cloud of steam. She didn't see him.

Grandmother had finished her washing. She was carrying her tub to the river's edge, swishing the clothes up and down, rinsing them in the clear water. There was Grandfather's shirt and his trousers and Grandmother's petticoat and her patchwork quilt and lace tablecloth. There was her red skirt. How carefully Grandmother rinsed her beautiful red skirt. She had made it for her seventy-seventh birthday. They had had a party. Grandmother had danced and danced and the red skirt had swirled around her ankles showing the little lace bows on her underslip. She had declared she didn't feel a day over seventeen and Grandfather had said, for sure she didn't look more than seventeen, either.

Oh, Grandmother loved that red skirt. She let it float out into the stream, the water splashed and danced over it making it swirl out just like it had on her seventy-seventh birthday. Grandmother was so busy remembering, her fingers loosed their hold. The river snatched the red skirt from Grandmother's hands. Too late she tried to pull it back. It floated and danced to the middle of the river out of her reach. Oh, no wonder Grandmother screamed.

Joseph saw it coming, dancing and bobbing,

straight towards the stepping stones. He quickly reached out to stop it. Too quickly! He slipped. He sat down on the big flat boulder and the red skirt floated on.

The bear saw that red skirt. She saw it twirling and dancing in the foam. Perhaps she thought it was a fish, a big, red sturgeon leaping over the waves, anyway she quickly shot out her paw and flipped Grandmother's red skirt out of the water. It flopped over her head on to her back.

Now Mother and Grandmother and Aunt Lyddie came running. They had seen what that bear had done. They had seen how she had saved Grandmother's red skirt. And right at that very minute here came Father and Grandfather and Uncle Isaac thinking with all that commotion going on someone was drowning for sure. It was quite a long time before they could understand what had happened, Mother and Aunt Lyddie were talking so fast and so loud, both trying to tell the story at the same time.

But Grandmother was so breathless from running, so trembling at the thought of losing

her red skirt and so happy and excited at getting it back that she could not say a word.

Joseph didn't say a word either. He was thinking, now if he had saved Grandmother's red skirt – if only he hadn't slipped when he reached to save it. How pleased Grandmother would be with him. How excitedly Mother and Aunt Lyddie would be telling Father and Grandfather and Uncle Isaac how clever he was. How proud Father would be of him. Why, Father might be so proud he might say— Father might say – he might— Joseph didn't dare think any further than that.

At last Grandmother stopped trembling. She got her breath back. She said: 'What should I have done if I'd lost my red skirt? That wonderful bear! That clever bear! How quickly she grabbed it, and so gentle, not a torn stitch or a tear or a scratch on it.' And Grandmother held up her red skirt to the light looking it over. Then she went up to the bear and patted her big, shaggy head.

Grandmother smiled at Joseph. She said, 'What a good thing you and that bear were on the stepping stones just at that moment.'

Grandmother looked hard at Grandfather and Uncle Isaac. She said, 'I do declare I never did see a more sensible animal than that bear.'

Then Grandmother looked sternly at Father. She said, 'I shouldn't be surprised if that bear turns out to be the most useful animal on the whole settlement.'

Father started to say something but Grandmother quickly said, 'I guess we'll all be glad Joseph's got a bear for a pet,' and she frowned quite fiercely at Father. She never could quite forget Father was not still her little boy.

Father looked at the bear. He looked at Joseph. He looked back at the bear and back again at Joseph. He looked at Grandmother frowning at him. He stroked his chin. 'Well,' he said at last, 'well, I guess you can keep that bear for a bit, Joseph. But just you mind she doesn't worry the stock or frighten the children. And when winter comes— If food gets scarce— '

Father didn't say any more, but Joseph knew what he meant and he was sure that this year winter wouldn't be too hard and there would be more than enough food for everyone, even his bear.

Chapter Seven

Snowfall

ONE day when Joseph was taking the bear across the meadows a group of cows came up curiously to look at her. Their wide inquisitive staring made the bear nervous, she stood up on her hind legs, waving her front paws and that made the cows nervous, too. At once they turned about, they kicked up their heels, they lowered their heads, they raced away with their tails in the air.

From the other end of the meadow the calves saw their mothers running. They rushed over to see what all the excitement was about and to join in. They were not very big but there were a lot of them. Their little pounding hooves sounded like thunder. The ground shook. They were coming so fast there was no time to get

out of the way. Straight for Joseph and the bear they came. Too fast to stop. On they came faster and faster. Joseph trembled to see all those calves charging down on him. He closed his eyes. He clung to the bear. Louder and louder sounded those little pounding hooves. Closer and closer they came. Just in time those calves saw that big bear. But they didn't stop. They couldn't. They swerved aside and raced on down the meadow.

No one was hurt. Joseph wasn't hurt. The bear wasn't hurt. But, oh, they were scared. Well, after that there was no need for Father to worry about the stock. The bear wouldn't even go near them. She wouldn't so much as put a foot in the meadow.

There was no need for Father to worry about the children either. The bear loved the children. She loved people. But most of all she loved Joseph. Every day he curried and brushed her until her coat shone. He never had her on a chain and soon the sore places on her neck and legs healed, her coat grew thick and long and you couldn't even see where they had been.

She followed Joseph everywhere, even to school. Now more than ever he wished he was clever enough to sit at the top of the class – in the seat by the window so that he could look out and see his bear patiently waiting for him to take her to the woods where the ground was thick with acorns and nuts and the trees and bushes were loaded down with fruit and berries.

While the bear filled herself with nuts and fruit Joseph filled a sack with beech nuts and cob nuts and shiny, brown chestnuts and acorns. He was getting in a store of food for her for winter.

He had ten sacks stored in the barn with the hay when the first frosts came. Ten sacks were not enough to last all winter. Joseph remembered what Father had said about not letting the stock go hungry to feed a bear and he hurried to fill more and more sacks. But by now the trees were bare and the ground so thick with fallen leaves that he could hardly find the nuts buried beneath them.

There were four more sacks in the barn when it started to snow, and for a while Joseph stopped worrying about his bear's winter feed.

Out came the toboggans and the little bobsleds and every hour of daylight was filled with shouts and laughter and flying snowballs. It was glorious.

Then more snow fell and more and more and still more. It piled in great drifts against the walls, even above the windows and it was so dark indoors that they had to have a candle burning all day. It crept under the doors and melted in little puddles along the sills. Snowflakes floated down the chimney and fell hissing and spluttering into the leaping flames. And all the time the wind whistled and howled and screamed at them.

Father said it was the worst blizzard he could remember. He said he knew now why nature had provided them with such a rich harvest in the fall, and he was glad they had found room to store all the extra crops.

Joseph went happy to bed that night. He thought then Father would not mind sharing the animals' feed with his bear and in the morning he gave her an extra dipper of nuts for breakfast.

Chapter Eight

The End of Winter

THE blizzard stopped at last but it was still icy cold. Their breath froze almost as soon as it came out of their mouths. The fun had gone out of tobogganing and the snow was too hard for snowballing. Cold and ice and winter stretched endlessly ahead. Spring seemed too far away even to think of.

In the forest the wild bears were sleeping winter away in hollow trees and mountain caves, and Joseph's bear spent her time happily curled up on a pile of straw in a corner of the wood shed. She ate very little. But in the big barn the cows and horses and pigs seemed never to stop eating.

Father began to look anxiously at the dwindling store of winter feed. He never mentioned

the bear but Joseph knew that in a shortage she would be the first to go hungry and at dinner time he took a doughnut or a piece of bread from his plate for her. Only Grandmother noticed and remembering her red skirt gave Joseph an extra helping of apple cake for supper.

At last the worst of winter was over. Every day the sun crept up a little higher in the sky. The days grew longer, drops of water sparkled on the ends of the icicles hanging from the roofs and began to drip monotonously. The trees shook off the snow from their branches and before long little islands of green appeared in the white meadows.

Pretty soon the animals could be turned out in the day-time to graze, but there was no goodness in the soggy grass. They still needed their feed of hay and grain.

And now the bear began to get restless, she smelt spring, she no longer wanted to spend the day cosily in the wood shed. She was into everything. She was a nuisance.

Mother grumbled, 'That bear keeps coming into my kitchen.'

Aunt Lyddie fretted, 'That bear nearly knocked me over.'

Even Grandmother complained, 'That bear is more trouble than she's worth.'

Father shouted at her, Grandfather scolded her and Uncle Isaac was for ever shooing her away from the school house window. She would peer in. Uncle Isaac was cross. He said to Joseph, 'I will not have that bear peering in the window. How can anyone do lessons with

a bear peering in the window? Take her away
and lock her in the wood shed.'

Joseph took the bear to the wood shed, but
he didn't lock her in. He left the door open a
crack for the air to get in. He didn't for one
minute think about the bear opening that crack
wider and getting out, and that was a good
thing because if he had thought about it he
would have shut the door tight and the bear
wouldn't have been able to get out, and then
who knows what terrible thing would have
happened!

Chapter Nine

The Snake

As soon as Joseph left her the bear came to the door. She saw the crack where the air came through. She put her nose to the crack and sniffed. She sniffed the fresh smells coming into the wood shed. She wriggled her nose, sniffing harder. Maybe she smelled little Jessie playing in the raspberry thicket where Mother was collecting young dandelion leaves for supper or maybe she just liked the way the cool air tickled her warm nose. Anyway she went on sniffing, harder and harder, wriggling and wriggling her nose until she had made that crack a big, wide open space and the good-outdoor smells were all around her.

Straight away off she lumbered to the raspberry thicket. Mother and little Jessie heard her coming, the dry twigs cracking beneath her heavy feet, the branches slapping back behind her as she pushed her way through the undergrowth.

Little Jessie laughed with delight and ran to meet her, she was tired of playing by herself. She was so pleased to see that big bear lolloping towards her she didn't see a big snake coiled under one of the raspberry bushes. She didn't see the tangled roots on the ground and caught her foot in them. Down she went, sprawling right beside the very raspberry bush that big snake was coiled under.

Like lightning the snake uncoiled itself, like a flash it slithered towards little Jessie, like poisoned arrows its long forked tongue shot in and out of its flat head.

Now little Jessie saw the snake. Mother saw the snake. They were filled with fear but they couldn't move or scream or cry out, they could only stare and listen to its angry rattling.

Now the bear saw the snake. She stood up on her hind legs. How big she was, how tall!

The snake paused preparing to strike. It

seemed to be licking its lips. It paused too long. Down crashed the bear. Like a rock one of her paws smashed that snake's great flat head. For a second its long body squirmed and wriggled and wildly thrashed the ground – and was still!

Now Mother came to life. She rushed to little Jessie, she picked her up and hugged her. She ran to the bear. She threw her arms round the bear's neck and kissed her. She laughed and cried at the same time she was so happy. She put little Jessie on the bear's back and led her to the settlement.

That bear almost had to run to keep up with Mother she was in such a hurry to tell everyone how Joseph's bear had saved little Jessie from the snake.

Chapter Ten

The Black Bear

THE bear had saved Grandmother's red skirt and that was something. But now she had saved little Jessie from the snake and that was wonderful. No talk of sending her away now. Joseph was so happy he couldn't believe it. It was too good to be true.

Now everyone loved that bear, they couldn't do enough for her, they fussed over her and petted her. She had so much food she almost couldn't eat it all. But still she was restless, still she was a nuisance. Now no one noticed – except Joseph. He worried. She was not the same. She no longer sat patiently while he curried her thick coat, rolling on to her back for him to brush the soft fur on her fat stomach. She was impatient, for ever prowling up and down, lifting her head, sniffing the wind and making little grumbling noises deep down in her throat.

One early morning Joseph went to the maple grove with Father to collect the sticky, sweet sap from the maple trees. Father was driving a wooden peg in the trunks of the trees and hanging a pail on it to catch the sap that oozed out. When the pails were full Joseph emptied them into a big pot for Mother to make sugar and syrup.

He was emptying one of the pots now when he glanced down and saw the prints – BEAR PRINTS! Straightaway he was uneasy. He looked back to where his bear was happily licking the sticky sap spilling down the bark of one of the trees.

Joseph hung the emptied pail back on its peg and went to collect another one from the next tree. Here were more prints, all round the base of the trunk, crossing and recrossing each other, coming from the direction of the forest. Now he really was worried. He looked back again at his bear, she was still scraping the sap

with her long rough tongue. She hadn't come this far into the grove yet. They couldn't be her prints. He gazed about him anxiously, he was growing more and more uneasy.

Father came up. 'What's the matter, son? What's wrong?' He took one look at the prints. 'Bears,' he said. 'I've never known them come this far down from the hills, especially this time of the year.' He bent down, examining them closely. 'It's just one bear. The prints are all the same. Now why would—?'

Joseph's bear ambled up. She sat on her haunches licking her sticky paws. At the same time there was a crashing, splintering sound in front of them. The bushes parted and a huge, black bear stood looking at them with tiny dangerous eyes. Father and Joseph stared back. For a second they couldn't move.

Out of the corner of his eye Joseph saw Father reaching for his rifle. He could feel his bear quivering beside him, hear her making little whimpering noises as though she were talking to that big, fierce, black bear. And then he knew – suddenly in that second Joseph

understood why his bear had been so restless lately. She had sensed this big strange bear was down here at the foot of the hills and all the wild instincts hidden for so long deep inside her were drawing her to him. As spring had come bringing new life to the cold earth so it had come to Joseph's bear, in the air, on the wind, in bird song and distant sounds of far away wild creatures. Spring had come and wakened in his bear a longing to be free.

Once he had taken her to the forest, offered her her freedom, but she had come back. He had thought her stupid then. But then he hadn't loved her as he did now so that the very thought of her going away was like a big ache inside him.

Father raised his rifle. Joseph held his breath. In a second Father would fire. In a second that black bear would be dead and wouldn't be able to take his bear away from him. She would forget the wild instincts that called her, she would come back to the settlement and live with him for ever.

Father was taking aim. His finger was on the trigger. Joseph's fingers tightened and locked in his bear's thick fur. There was a pain in his throat. 'No, Father,' he whispered. He loosed his fingers. At once his bear darted forward. Straight to that big black bear. She nuzzled his ear, they rubbed noses, they turned around and quickly lumbered off through the trees. The bushes closed behind them.

Father lowered his rifle. He didn't say a word, he didn't look at Joseph. He picked up the big pot of maple sap and Joseph helped him carry it back to Mother.

Uncle Isaac was ringing the school bell, clanging and clanging it because Joseph was late. Father stopped to talk to him while Joseph went to wash his sticky hands at the pump.

Uncle Isaac stopped ringing the bell. Joseph made his way to the back of the school room. Cousin Hannah was sitting in his seat. He shuffled his feet, looking at the floor. He didn't

know what to do, he was confused and un-happy. He wanted to cry.

Uncle Isaac put his hand on Joseph's shoulder. He said gently, 'There are many kinds of lessons to be learned, Joseph, not all of them from books. Sometimes it is more important to be wise than clever. Go and sit down, boy, at the top of the class – in the seat by the window.'

TALES FROM
ALLOTMENT LANE SCHOOL
Margaret Joy

A collection of twelve lively stories set in the reception class of a primary school. Miss Mee and her mixed class of five-year-olds have a series of day-to-day experiences, which make extremely entertaining and humorous reading.

THREE CHEERS FOR RAGDOLLY ANNA
Jean Kenward

Made only from a morsel of this and a tatter of that, Ragdolly Anna is a very special doll. Her adventures were serialised for television.

HAIRY AND SLUG
Margaret Joy

Meet Slug, a battered old car with a personality, and Hairy, an extremely shaggy mongrel addicted to television. They both belong to an ordinary family, with two children, and together they make up a hilarious combination of fun and adventure.

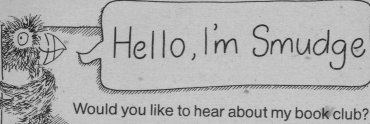

Hello, I'm Smudge

Would you like to hear about my book club?

It's for 4-8 year-olds and you get your own badge, membership book and a Club magazine four times a year.

MEMBERSHIP CARD

I BELONG TO THE JUNIOR PUFFIN CLUB

WELCOME

It's packed with stories, puzzles and competitions.

The Egg

You get a chance to buy new books!

And there's lots more! For further details and an application form send a stamped, addressed envelope to:

The Junior Puffin Club,
Penguin Books Limited,
Bath Road,
Harmondsworth,
Middlesex UB7 0DA